GLADIATOR BOY

THE REBELS' ASSAULT

GLADIATOR BOY

THE REBELS' ASSAULT

DAVID GRIMSTONE

*Hodder
Children's
Books*

A division of Hachette Children's Books

For Sebastian David Francesco Stone, my son.

I would like to dedicate the entire Gladiator Boy *series to Terry Pratchett. There is no writer, living or dead, for whom I have greater respect. Thank you for everything.*

CONTENTS

ANCIENT ITALY

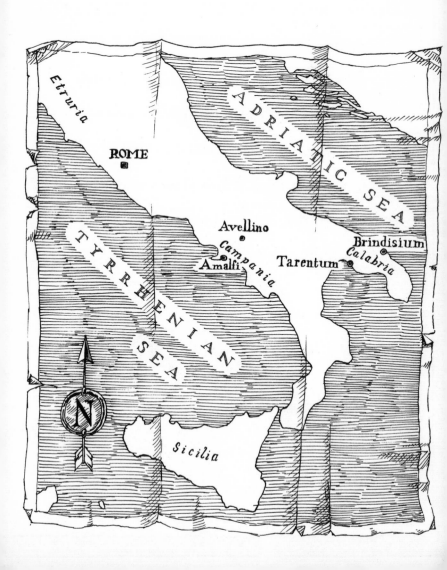

PREVIOUSLY IN GLADIATOR BOY

Decimus Rex and Olu fled Arena Primus and managed to escape the clutches of Drin Hain, Slavious Doom's shadowy apprentice. After following a grimy path through the sewers, they managed to sneak aboard a ship. Unfortunately, their fellow slaves were not so lucky. Ruma, Argon, Teo and Gladius are all still in the power of Slavious Doom . . .

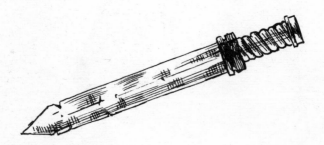

CHAPTER
I

THE
CHOOSING

Ruma, Argon, Teo and Gladius were led down from their cell at the top of Suvius Tower, dragged by the jailer's guards with such force that several cuts and bruises were earned along the way. At one point, Gladius stumbled and fell headlong down a flight of steps in the tower courtyard. However, rather than stop his momentum, the guards simply laughed and one even gave him an experimental kick to see if he would keep going. By the time the group reached the gates of the fortress they had stored up enough hatred for their captors to last several lifetimes.

In the courtyard, an eerie silence reigned. The guards assembled the slave line with a series of grunts and shoves. Then they withdrew, making space for the arrival of the spindly, gnome-like jailer who had so gleefully given the prisoners news of their pending executions. He climbed a wooden ladder beside the gates and hurried along a platform that spanned the gap just under the great archway. The slave line followed his progress and their eyes came to rest on the recognizable form of Drin Hain, draped in his trademark black robes and hood. The jailer cupped a hand to his face and whispered something to the wraith-like figure.

Hain unfolded his arms and addressed the slaves.

'As you know, Lord Doom and myself are both very fond of games. You will now be given the chance to choose the order and manner of your executions.' He pointed a finger at Gladius. 'YOU first.'

The slave looked up at Hain nervously, his eyes moving from the dark assassin to the jailer and then along the platform. However, there was no indication of the task he was being ordered to perform. The rest of the platform was clear and, apart from the assembled group and the guards, the courtyard was empty.

The jailer motioned to the guard at Gladius's side.

'Show him the way.'

Before Gladius could even turn to face the direction the jailer had indicated, he was slammed in the shoulder and almost knocked to the ground. He managed to right himself

at the last instant, and quickly side-stepped a second assault before waddling backwards with his hands held protectively in front of his face.

There was no further explanation given

and, at first, Ruma, Teo and Argon all thought that Gladius would actually have to fight the guard. They were all taken aback when the big man suddenly lowered his spear.

Gladius stopped dead; he didn't have much choice, seeing as he was now backed against the base of the tower.

'Wh-what do I have to do?' he asked, when the guard made no further move to attack him.

The silence continued, but the guard lowered his eyes to a point level with Gladius's knees and nodded an indication.

Gladius looked down, and then stepped away from a large, circular grate in the tower wall.

'In there?' he said, tentatively. 'Y-you want me to go in there?'

Drin Hain's voice rang out across the courtyard like a crack of thunder.

'You will descend the stone chute and swim through the submerged tunnel. At the far end is a deep well and in that well, fastened to a sunken statue of the mighty Jupiter, are four golden torcs. Each of these neck-bands has a value, ranging from the very expensive to the utterly worthless. Retrieve one, and one only. Then return to the entrance tunnel and call for us – a rope will then be lowered. Do not linger, for your friends will be made to stand in the baking sun until you return. You may begin.'

Much to the surprise of the assembled slaves, Gladius didn't even pause: he simply turned, wrenched open the grate and plunged into the darkness beyond.

A rush of air shocked the breath from him as he slipped and slid down the slimy stone chute with alarming speed, the glistening green walls rushing past him.

He cried out, a wail that echoed throughout the entire courtyard and caused several of the guards to snigger, before landing with a heavy splash in a vertical tunnel beneath the tower.

Realizing that the tunnel was a lot deeper than he had expected, Gladius immediately began to kick with all his might. At length, he broke the crest of the water, sucking in a deep breath and trying to paddle on the spot.

The opening through which he'd fallen was far above him; well beyond his reach. The only viable exit was an adjoining, equally flooded channel that stretched off in an easterly direction.

Gladius took in another deep lungful of the tunnel's fetid air, and dived under the water.

A murky vista greeted Gladius when he managed to force his eyes open. The channel seemed to go on for about ten metres before turning left. As there didn't seem to be any breathing space in this section of tunnel, Gladius swam with all his strength in order to reach the bend. Then, bringing his arms tightly to his sides, he propelled himself along the new channel. The statue was visible now, standing at the end of the tunnel with weeds and other marine growths swirling around it. Gladius could just make out the golden glint of the torcs, which were all fastened around the statue's neck.

He dived
deeper into
the tunnel
using blocks
of sunken
masonry to
help his progress.

Down. Down. Down.

His fingers found the statue, but already
he could feel the exhalation building inside
him. There was no TIME to study the torcs,
no TIME to do anything but snatch one,
unfasten it and then swim frantically for the
entrance tunnels and its glorious oasis of
breathing space.

Gladius reached out a hand and took hold
of the first torc he could reach. His chest

now ready to explode, he swooped and turned in the water, propping his feet against the statue and pulling at the neck ring with all his strength. The torc came away from the stone with surprising ease, and Gladius began to swim madly for the entrance tunnel, kicking himself off the statue and spearing through the water. He spluttered, water flooding into his mouth and nostrils as he began to panic, flailing madly as he tried to drive himself back along the original channel. A terrible fear gripped him as the tension in his lungs grew, and he felt closer to death than he had done throughout the trials that Slavious Doom's hideous servants had set for him.

He put on one last burst of speed, and

powered on. Unfortunately, Gladius was still too far from the entrance well . . . and his strength was leaving him.

A series of grey images flashed before his eyes; downcast faces and cruel, cackling masks. He saw Ruma, Argon and Teo all sharing his fate: a watery grave that swallowed them all one by one. He saw Slavious Doom and Drin Hain, both drinking wine and smiling down at the lifeless corpses of the slaves. He saw Decimus Rex . . .

. . . who had taken on the arena, and triumphed.

In the roasting courtyard, an uncomfortable silence had descended on the slave line. They were all thinking the same, dreadful thought: Gladius was too heavy to swim a network of flooded channels – he wasn't going to make it. Ruma risked a glance at Hain, who was still occupying the platform over the arched gate. The cloaked assassin showed no signs of concern; his arms were still folded and his rigid stance had not altered in the slightest. Beside him, however, the jailer was darting furtive looks at the heavy-set guard who'd marched Gladius to the opening. He was obviously of the opinion that Gladius had drowned in the waters beneath the tower.

As Ruma turned to face his companions, Argon lowered his head: even Teo looked away. Poor, clumsy Gladius had fallen before his method of execution had even been decided.

'Maybe it's better this way,' Ruma muttered. 'For Gladius, I mean: he would never have—'

'Out! OUT! Ouuuuuuut!'

The cry echoed across the courtyard, causing several guards to start and all the slaves to leap back in surprise. There was a half-second pause before Gladius's voice pierced the silence again.

'I have a torc! Lower the rope!'

The guard nearest the grate turned to Hain, who gave a quick nod of permission. Dropping his spear, he hurried over to a length of rope that was secured on an iron ring at the base of the tower wall. Then he heaped it on to his shoulder and, arriving at the grate, lowered the slack into the gloomy darkness below.

When Gladius finally emerged, puffing, panting and soaking wet, from the grate, none of the slaves could stop themselves from smiling . . . especially when he flopped over on to the baking sand and lay there like a beached whale, spitting out plumes of water as the guards advanced on him.

'Well?' Hain yelled, as the jailer scurried down the ladder and hurried across the courtyard. 'Which torc does he have?'

One of the guards reached down and drew the necklace from the slave's unresisting grip. However, it was quickly snatched by the jailer, who practically fell over himself in his determined dash to place it in Hain's gloved hands.

'This torc is the most finely crafted of those we placed below,' the assassin decreed. 'Therefore, Gladius has earned the right to be executed by my OWN hand.'

Ruma gasped, while Argon and Teo shared a horrified glance.

On the sand, Gladius raised his head slightly, and stared at the distant shape of the

man who would end his life: the icy depths of
the well would have provided a preferable
end.

Hain beckoned to the jailer and pointed
at Argon, who was next in line.

'My turn, then,' Argon muttered, as
Gladius was dragged back to the line
and dumped unceremoniously on to
the hot ground.

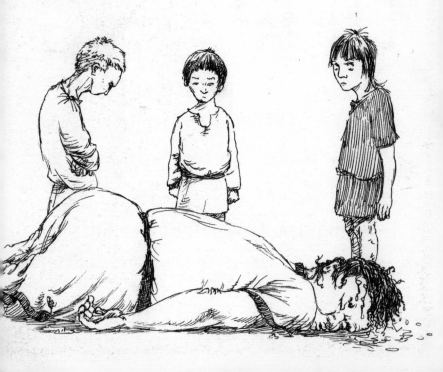

CHAPTER
II

THE
UPRISING

The *Caveat* rocked back and forth on the rolling ocean. In the depths of the ship, Decimus and Olu were both feeling incredibly sick, but the crew were used to the rhythmic pitching of the deck and their slaves were so exhausted that any mere sickness would have been a luxury. However, Decimus and Olu weren't simply sick because of the ocean – they were recovering from shock. A few seconds before, a trapdoor had been flung open and a dead slave had been cast down into their hiding place, thrown aside like a used rag and left to rot.

However, the slave deck itself didn't have many better sights to offer.

A scarred brute of a man stalked between

the rowers, barking abuse
and stopping
occasionally to whip
those that he felt
weren't pulling their
weight. This amounted

to just about anyone who wasn't already
bleeding and occasionally the odd
unfortunates who were already bleeding, and
had stopped rowing briefly to try to staunch
the flow of blood from their backs.

Arriving beside the smallest slave on the
deck, the hulking crewman raised his whip
and grinned. The victim rowed for all he was
worth, throwing what little strength he had
into the gesture. Unfortunately, it made no
difference: the whip came down upon him,

birthing a glistening line of blood on his back as the little man cried out in pain.

The brute was about to follow his attack with a second strike, when another crewman appeared at the entrance to the deck. This one was shorter and had a single eye: the other was covered by a rough patch of skin. His hair was long and matted, and he walked with a stoop.

'What do you want?' the brute boomed, lowering his whip as the second crewman approached.

'Keys,' said the one-eyed slaver. 'Captain reckons we're turning too fast.' He cast a glance around the deck. 'And it's your fault.'

'Yeah? How d'you work that out?'

'Because you've put a stronger crew on

the port side. We need to swap some of 'em over.'

The big crewman looked around at the heaving slave lines, and nodded.

'Better get the keys, then,' he said.

'Are you deaf? I came to get them from you. Captain says you took 'em this morning.'

'I didn't; haven't moved anyone around so I never needed 'em. Maybe one of the others has 'em?'

The one-eyed slaver nodded. 'Who did you take over from?'

'Barius.'

'I'll go and ask 'im.'

The brute waited until the little crewman had disappeared, and then he turned back to the slave who was still cowering before him.

'You didn't think I'd forget, did you?' he growled, raising the whip once again.

Olu had been in the bilge all morning, trying hard not to be sick. He and Decimus had argued long and hard about which of them should sneak into the captain's cabin and steal the keys; Decimus had won. Olu was quicker on his feet, but Decimus was stronger. At least if Decimus was caught he might stand a chance; Olu was still far too exhausted to fight anyone. Besides, the young warrior was BORN lucky: the arena trials had proved that. Olu himself had a far simpler but equally dangerous task ahead: he would have to distract the crew so that Decimus could free the slaves.

The ship lurched suddenly, and Olu felt his stomach churn. He steadied himself on a barrel, and tried to breathe. It was no good: he still felt dreadful.

Decimus appeared at the entrance hatch and quickly scrambled down the ladder.

'I've got them,' he said, hurrying over to Olu and rattling the ring of iron keys. 'The captain's asleep – I think he might be a BIG drinker. I sneaked around for a bit, and got a decent look over the ship. I was lucky, though – at one point I thought one of the deckhands had seen me.'

Olu coughed, still clutching at his stomach. 'So what are we dealing with?'

'The crew is pretty standard,' said Decimus. 'There are four working the deck and two on the sails. The one who runs the slaves is a real animal; must be bigger than a wild bear. There's also an oily little wretch with one eye who seems to run around barking orders and getting in everyone's way.'

'And that's all of them, is it?' Olu hazarded. 'The entire crew?'

'Yeah; I think so. Are you ready?'

The slave whistled between his teeth, and nodded.

'As ready as I'll ever be.'

The hulking brute proceeded along the line, occasionally lowering his whip and actually driving a fist into the faces of the exhausted slaves. He was reaching the end of the deck when the little one-eyed crewman reappeared, limping towards him with a mirthless expression on his weathered features.

'You MUST have those keys,' he snapped. 'I've spoken to Barius and he told me he put them back in the captain's cabin.'

'And?'

'And they're not there now, so where are they?'

'You saying I've got 'em when I haven't, you little runt?'

The one-eyed slaver shook his fist angrily

in the brute's face.

'I'm saying you're a stinking no-good liar who just made me search all round the ship for no good reason. Now hand over those—'

His voice spluttered into silence, partly because the big man had seized him around

the throat but mostly because a collective gasp had gone up from the slaves ranked along both sides of the ship.

The two crewmen followed the shocked gazes of their prisoners to the hatch at the end of the deck, where a young boy had appeared and was standing in the centre aisle with a determined but sickly smile on his face.

'If you want your keys,' he said, his voice ringing out in the stunned silence.

'You're gonna have to move REALLY fast.' Without another word, he turned on his heels, dashed across the slave line and scrambled up the ladder that led on to the deck.

Still clutching each other and staring wildly, the two crewmen slowly came to their senses and began to give chase, screaming at the top of their voices and falling over one another in a clumsy attempt to pursue the stowaway.

The slaves stopped rowing en masse, and watched as their captors struggled at the base of the ladder, the big brute shoving his smaller colleague aside at the last minute.

A roar of laughter from the slaves drew contemptuous glares from both men, before the big brute gained the advantage and climbed up towards the deck.

His companion snarled after him, but

sensibly left a few seconds before giving pursuit.

When both the slavers had crawled out of view, slamming the trapdoor behind them, and the noise above become an unbearable din, a second boy appeared. This one was a carrying a heavy ring of iron keys that looked all too familiar.

A sudden excitement washed through the room, as Decimus Rex set to work on the end of the line, casting chain after chain to the floor . . . and giving forty bruised and bleeding slaves their freedom.

Olu scampered across the deck, spotting a short plank of mostly rotted wood that was propped against a barrel and snatching it up as he ran. When he was halfway across the deck, he suddenly took a detour and dashed for a sturdy-looking rope ladder that was secured to the mast.

As crewmen all over the ship were alerted by the cries of the pursuing slavers, Olu magnified the chaos by screaming at the top of his voice and slamming the wooden plank against the mast. Within seconds, he had the attention of every man on the *Caveat*, including the captain who had emerged, blinking, from his cabin. Olu took one sweeping glance at the attention his handiwork had drawn, and then he shot up the rope ladder, moving so fast that two of the crew actually ran into each other in an attempt to catch him.

'Get him!' the captain thundered, striding over the deck as the crew of the *Caveat* scattered around him. 'Dead or alive, I want that boy brought DOWN!'

Olu climbed higher, reaching the first platform before peering down to see who was following him. It seemed that most of the crew had an issue with heights; only the oily, one-eyed pirate from the slave deck had followed him up the ladder. The little man was surprisingly quick, too: he was already halfway up, a dagger pressed firmly between his teeth.

'If you don't bring that boy down here,' the captain yelled from the deck, 'you needn't bother coming down yourself!'

Olu looked up at the next platform, and down at his frantic pursuer.

Come on, Decimus, he thought. I'm not like you – I can't do this stuff all on my own . . .

Then a roar went up from below . . . and the hatch to the slave deck exploded outwards.

CHAPTER III

WAR!

A crowd of more than a hundred
merchants gathered in the
courtyard of Suvius Tower.
A large, flat scaffold had been
erected, supporting a grand
stage that was overlooked
by a balcony that
jutted from the
tower like a great
jaw. Standing on
the balcony,
surveying the crowd,
were Slavious Doom and Drin Hain, deep in
conversation.

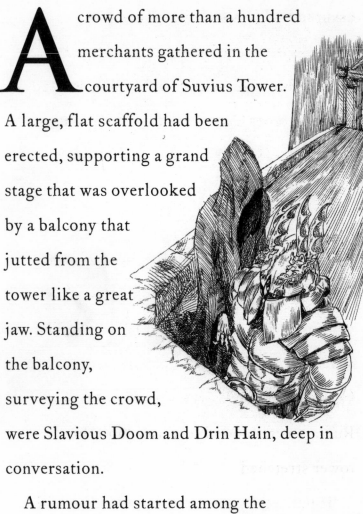

A rumour had started among the
merchants that Doom had only graced the
event with his presence because he had been

assured by Hain that the planned executions would draw out the escaped slaves whose faces adorned so many wanted posters across Campania. One thing was certain: an air of excitement was swirling among the growing crowd, eager to see the promised executions.

In the highest room of the Suvius Tower, Ruma stared through a large, barred window at the drama unfolding below. The crowd looked like a hive of insects swarming before a great mound: once again, Ruma was reminded just how high the tower stretched.

'It practically pierces the clouds,' he said aloud, '... and, sometime in the next hour, I'm going to be thrown from the top of it.

How LUCKY am I?'

'Luckier than me,' Argon snarled, practically spitting the words out. 'At least you can avoid being ripped apart by – what was it? – oh yes: lions, crocodiles or snakes. Only, I don't get to know which ones until I actually drop into their lair.' He kicked at the rough stone wall of the cell. 'That's OK, though – because it doesn't matter what I get: I'm absolutely terrified of them all.'

'You'd rather be hung like Teo, would you?' Ruma snapped, indicating the slave who sat, uncomplaining, in the corner of the cell. 'I suppose you think he's got it easy?'

'I'll tell you who has got it easy,' the Gaul growled, turning his attention to the slumbering form of Gladius. 'Gladius, that's who. Dispatched by the sword? It's not exactly going to be long and drawn out, is it? Hain is probably so quick he won't even see the end coming. And why? Just because he got lucky and picked the right necklace . . .'

'We mustn't turn on each other,' Ruma warned, moving through the room to stand between Argon and Gladius. He took several deep breaths to calm himself. 'That's exactly what Doom and Hain want.'

'Rubbish,' said Argon, dismissively. 'All Doom wants is to capture Decimus and Olu. Our deaths are nothing but bait . . . well, that and entertainment for his bloated merchant friends.'

'He'll come back,' said Gladius, quietly. It was the first time he had spoken since the trial of the torcs. All eyes turned toward him.

'You what?' Argon prompted. 'Did you actually say something worth listening to?'

'Decimus will come back,' Gladius repeated. 'I know I've been pretty mean about him since he escaped, but that's just because I was angry that we didn't get away, too. I know what sort of person Decimus is. He'll come here, and give himself up.'

'Yeah,' said Ruma, doubtfully, returning to the window and squinting down at the courtyard. 'Well I hope he picks up some speed, because it looks to me like the executioners are ready.'

The *Caveat* was hosting a war. More than half the ship's complement of abused and starving slaves had broken against the bewildered crew like a tidal wave washing over a beach. Despite the fact that most of the captain's men were armed, they were quickly overpowered by the sheer weight of numbers. The remaining slaves had accompanied Decimus to the cabin, where swords, shields and a variety of brass knuckles and mailed gauntlets had been acquired.

The slavers themselves were being shown as much mercy as they had previously awarded their prisoners. Several were dispatched by the sword, while others were simply thrown over the side of the ship. The

captain had drawn his own blade and was

being backed to the starboard side of the

deck by a group of heavily scarred slaves

intent on providing him with a painful death. A short distance away, the hulking brute who'd so gleefully whipped and beaten the prisoners in his care was now being introduced to a world of tar and flames: his agonized screams echoed all over the ship, until he stumbled overboard and the ocean claimed him.

Far above the developing chaos, Olu was struggling with the oily-haired, one-eyed crewman. The little man had caught up with the slave in the crow's nest and, after exchanging several heavy blows, both of them had fought for control of the crewman's dagger. Fortunately, Olu had managed to force the weapon out of his enemy's grip, sending it spearing towards the deck below.

Now they were even or, Olu reflected, as even as they were ever likely to be.

A punch knocked the slave back against the top of the mast, momentarily winding him. One thing was certain: the little man was deceptively strong. Olu ducked a second punch and the one-eyed slaver's bloodied knuckles glanced off the wood. He made to deliver a kick of his own, but the attempt was swiftly blocked and the slaver snatched hold of his neck instead.

Throwing his considerable strength into the fight, the crewman drove Olu back to the edge of the crow's nest, his iron grip still closed upon the young slave's neck.

Olu felt his back press firmly against the wooden rail, and knew he only had one chance against the wily sailor. Dropping to his knees, he used every ounce of his own energy to drag the little man on to his back and hoist him over the edge of the rail.

'Whatyaaahhahaahahaahhahaahahahahah!'

The high-pitched scream from the slaver was abruptly cut off as he plummeted to his death.

Away from the explosive confusion, Decimus Rex had climbed on to the higher galley, where two of the stronger and more

agile slaves were wrestling with the ship's wheel.

Decimus cupped a hand around his mouth and yelled across the deck, continuing to belt out his drowned words even as the rioting ceased and the drunken wretch of a captain was dumped over the side of the ship.

'. . . en to me!' Decimus finished. The assembled slaves now turned their attention to the young warrior and his nimble companion now climbing down the mast to join him. 'Please! Listen to me! My name is Decimus Rex and, like you, I am a slave! I come from Arena Primus, where Slavious Doom had my friends and me imprisoned to pay off the debts of our parents! My friend Olu and I escaped his grasp, and now our faces appear on scrolls throughout the continent! Our time is limited and our fates are all but sealed. Nevertheless, we have released you all today: not only to give you your freedom, but to ask – no, to BEG you – for help!'

As Olu finally reached the upper galley, he saw that Decimus had drawn the attention of the entire slave gathering. Every eye was upon him, and all of the men seemed to be listening with a mixture of wild confusion and gratitude.

'In a tower,' Decimus continued, pointing towards the land-mass that was now clearly visible from the starboard side of the ship, 'that I believe stands just along the coast from here, four of our friends are about to be put to death.' He raised an arm and gripped Olu by the shoulder. 'They are no older than myself and Olu, and have committed no crime except to be born to those less wealthy than the merchant classes! It is our plan to attack the tower, and to free our friends! We may not succeed, but we will try. I would not ask any of you to come with us ... but if you could suffer our company a while longer and get the ship to our destination, then Olu and I would be greatly in your debt. We ask this—'

Decimus tried to continue, but his voice was drowned out by a thunderous roar from the slaves. Instead, he turned to Olu and whispered, 'How far do you think we are from Suvius Tower?'

The slave smiled back at his friend, and pointed over Decimus's right shoulder.

'Unless I'm very much mistaken,' he said, 'that's it.'

CHAPTER IV

EXECUTION!

Afternoon arrived in southern Campania, though it failed to herald the arrival of even the slightest breeze. An unbearable heat haze had forced the land into submission: guards cooked in their armour without a word of complaint as their miserable masters were fanned with giant palm leaves, and a restlessness gripped those who were eager to be distracted.

A deathly silence stole over the merchant crowd as Slavious Doom appeared at the entrance to Suvius Tower and began the long climb to the base of the scaffold. Drin Hain trailed after the overlord, his black cloak billowing out behind him. Following the pair at a respectful distance was a small party of guards, and each one was dragging their own hooded prisoner.

As Argon, Teo and Gladius progressed along the scaffold, they could hear the shouts and jeers of the crowd all around them. Though the hoods prevented them from seeing the crowd or the scene that lay before them, the slaves were more consumed by their own fears than the thought of the eager, over-fed faces that would be gathered all around the courtyard, baying for their blood. Argon thought of his impending death in the cages that were undoubtedly ranged beneath the scaffold, Teo thought of the pit over which he would frantically struggle when the hangman's noose was placed around his neck, and Gladius could think only of the demonic figure of Drin Hain raising a curved sword and striking him down without the merest flinch of mercy. Far above the slaves, the courtyard and the scaffold itself, Ruma – the only slave whose head had not been covered with a cloth sack – surveyed the scene from the very top of Suvius Tower. His mind was galloping furiously, taking in the surrounding buildings, the guards at his side, the chains around him and the rising noise from the distant courtyard as his friends were sent towards their doom. He looked down and squinted at the scaffold: his friends were being separated.

Ruma's gaze shifted back to his chains as several of the guards departed, leaving a single large brute behind – presumably the

one who'd been given the task of throwing
him over the edge.

The chains, he thought, his eyes following
the links to a stout ring that was wedged in
the stone floor of the tower. You need a plan,
Ruma, and you need one NOW.

Slavious Doom's voice was unmistakable:
every word was roared yet spoken at the same
time, each syllable pronounced with
incredible accuracy. 'Merchant friends; you
are about to witness something special for
your entertainment on this day! Look
skyward, my friends, and you will see a small
figure on the very edge of the tower top. That

is Ruma, an Etrurian slave whose execution will start the proceedings. When Ruma has breathed his last, your attention will turn to THIS section of scaffold . . .' Doom raised his hand and pointed to a platform where Argon now stood before three large trapdoors. From their vantage point, the crowd could see two cages and a pit beneath the trapdoors; the cages contained lions and crocodiles, respectively, while the pit literally writhed with snakes. Argon could see nothing, even when the hood was ripped from his head.

'I give you a slave whose method of execution lies in his own hands,' Doom bellowed. 'I give you . . . Argon the Gaul!'

The crowd cheered wildly, but they were

once again shouted down by the commanding voice of their delighted host.

'When Argon has paid the highest price for his family's debt,' Doom continued, 'you will need to turn your eyes to the small stage at the centre of the scaffold . . . for there you will see a glorious sight indeed. Gladius, a Brindisium boy who has never missed a meal in his life – haha – will face in mortal combat my own dark apprentice: the assassin Drin Hain!'

A collective gasp went up from the merchants as the sack was removed from Gladius's face, revealing the young slave's look of apprehensive horror. Drin Hain was standing opposite him, brandishing the most evil-looking sword Gladius had ever seen.

The trembling slave glanced down at his feet; a short sword had been placed on the ground before him, and it looked functional at best.

Again, the crowd roared its approval.

'Finally,' Doom cried. 'We have Teo.' The executioners positioned Teo over a large trapdoor on a stage that was opposite to the ones containing Argon and Gladius. Once the

noose was firmly around the slave's neck, his hood was removed. 'Unless Gladius surprises us against the great Hain,' Doom went on, his voice now so edged with wicked excitement that he could barely contain his glee, 'Teo's trapdoor will open the second his fat friend is no more. Hahahaahhaahaha!'

The crowd exploded and Slavious Doom took a deep bow and signalled to one of the guards that it was time for the event to begin.

The guard bowed low, then walked out on to the centre of the scaffold, looked towards the top of the tower and raised a red flag.

Ruma saw the flag even before he felt the tower-top executioner shove him hard in the small of the back. However, he was more than prepared. Since his chains had been

unlocked, he'd gone
to great pains to
distract the guard by
hurling abuse and
goading the man
several times to hit
him. During these
distractions, Ruma
had curled a foot

around the chain that had been cast aside and
had managed to loop it twice around his ankle.
Now, as the guard moved forward to shove him
from the edge of the tower, he quickly spun
around and grabbed the man around the waist.
Caught unawares, the guard made a desperate
attempt to drive his knee into the slave's
stomach, but Ruma again used the strike to his

own advantage, looping the chain around the guard's raised leg before deliberately releasing his grip and letting all his muscles relax. Believing the slave's loss of energy was due to the force of his own strength, the guard grasped Ruma by the tattered rags he was wearing and quite literally hurled him over the edge of the tower. Distracted by the wild, whooping cheers from the crowd, he wasn't aware of the chain beginning to uncurl until it was far, far too late.

In the courtyard, every face was turned toward the top of Suvius Tower. A sudden, collective gasp of excitement and several cheers had greeted the sight of the young slave flying over the battlements and beginning his long plunge ... but the rounds of applause soon turned to cries of horror as Ruma hung, suspended by a long chain, approximately fifty feet from the tower-top. To make matters worse, one of Doom's guards had quickly followed him over and was himself suspended by the same chain some ten or twenty feet above the slave.

While most of the crowd were positively transfixed by the scenes unfolding on the lofty summit of Suvius, several fascinated glances were also being thrown at Slavious Doom, whose own face was a picture of furious outrage.

Unfortunately, Doom had no time to bark any further orders before the crowd were hit with a new and very unexpected episode in the unfolding drama of the first execution: the

guard managed to free his foot from the chain
... and he fell.

Ruma, still hanging with his foot locked
firmly in the chain, felt something rush past
him, but the half-horrified, half-elated
screams of the crowd drowned out the death-
cry of the guard as he plunged down, down,
down, twisting in the air, tumbling over and
over on the wind ... until ...

Some of the crowd looked away, and most of those that didn't still swiftly covered their eyes. For many the sound was even worse; a sudden and terrible crunch as the guard's  fractured and broken body slammed into the centre of the courtyard.

Slavious Doom was still fixated on the corpse when an unexpected and quite deafening cheer rose up from the merchants all around him.

Temporarily dazed by the events, Doom was still a consummate entertainer, and he quickly picked up on the feelings of his audience.

'A death is a death!' he screamed at the

pack of stunned servants who still gathered close to him. 'Move the Gaul to the trapdoors … NOW!'

The two guards holding Argon shoved him forward, choosing to ready their spears on the chance that the Gaul tried anything in the light of his companion's antics at the top of the tower.

'The Gaul!' Doom screamed with all his might, trying to pry the merchants' attention away from Ruma, who had managed to right himself and was now swinging back and forth on the chain with a determined sense of purpose that none of the awed crowd seemed able to predict. 'Drop the Gaul – NOW!'

Flustered, the guards threw down their spears and rushed Argon forward, choosing one of the trapdoors seemingly at random before hauling it open and throwing the Gaul in.

Despite the swift and clumsy handling of the move, it did seem to draw the crowd's attention, especially when it became apparent that the young slave had been thrown into the snake pit.

Assured that the focus of attention had been shifted away from Ruma, Slavious Doom turned immediately to one of his guards.

'Get up to the top of that tower and free the chain,' Doom growled. 'I don't care how you do it, just get it done, or you can die with the rest of the slaves. Understand?'

The guard nodded, and hurried away.

Slavious Doom watched him vanish through the door and then returned his gaze to the pit, where Argon had leapt to his feet and was slowly backing away from three hissing cobras that were advancing on the young slave in a series of twists and turns.

'Master—'

Doom glanced briefly at another guard who had scrambled up the scaffold to get to him.

'Wait.'

'B-but, Master—'

'Are you deaf? I told you to WAIT.'

Doom didn't take his eyes off the scene in the snake pit, and he wasn't the only one. The entire merchant crowd gasped and drew back their heads as one of the cobras darted

forward, missing Argon by a fraction of an
inch. The Gaul leapt into a new space,
dodging two shiny green snakes that reared
up at him as he tried to avoid the attentions

of a massive python slumbering in the near corner of the pit. Argon was staying light on his feet, but his mind was a black hole of despair: after all, it could only be a matter of time before one of them got him.

'Master? M-master?'

Slavious Doom slowly turned his head to face the spineless servant with the annoying voice who seemed intent on bothering him.

'If you say another word, I will have you KILLED. Do you underst—'

'We're under attack, Master!' The words were spluttered out. 'We're under attack!'

Doom's face froze for a moment, and then he spoke very slowly, turning the guard away from the gathered merchants as he did so. 'Where?' he muttered. 'And do speak quietly, for your life does depend upon your discretion.'

'The gate, Master.' A shaking finger was pointed back towards the entrance to the courtyard. 'A ship arrived. We thought it was a slaver, so two of the sentries went down to talk to 'em . . . but now they're dead, and there's an army of slaves heading for the main gates. There must be fifty of 'em!'

Slavious Doom signalled to a group of guards who were standing idly between the merchant crowd and the scaffold. They quickly marched over to join him.

'You will come with me to the main gate,' he said. Then, turning back to face the scaffold, Doom cupped his hands around his mouth and shouted at the top of his voice.

'Kill the other two slaves!' he cried. 'Now!'

As the wall of merchant faces focused on the brave Gaul who was dancing nimbly among the snakes, Slavious Doom turned and ran for the entrance.

Behind him, Drin Hain rushed headlong

at the still trembling Gladius, while Teo's trapdoor was quickly pulled out from under him, leaving him kicking in mid-air while the noose stretched his bony neck . . .

CHAPTER
V

THE
RESCUE

Decimus Rex saw Slavious Doom
approaching long before the
pair came face to face. He and
Olu had been ordered to the back of the line
by the *Caveat* slaves, who were so grateful for
their freedom that they had insisted on
leading the assault against Suvius Tower
without them. Decimus had quickly refused
the offer, but had nevertheless been held
back while the slaves, all armed with
cutlasses, made short work of the sentries on

guard at the tower. More guards had arrived, but none were a match for the slaves, who fought with a bloodlust born of the terrible treatment they had received on the *Caveat*.

Then, suddenly, everything had changed. The great doors of the courtyard had been thrown open and a new wave of guards flooded out. Among them was Slavious Doom.

Resplendent in his golden armour, the overlord of Arena Primus cut his way through the slave line like a man swatting away flies.

'We don't stand a chance,' Olu whispered. 'Look at him! The man is absolutely insane! If he finds out we're here—'

'He already knows,' Decimus interrupted.

'Don't ask me how, but he does. And you're right – we can't fight him. We need to use the slaves as a distraction and sneak around him. Otherwise, Gladius and the others are dead.'

'They're probably dead already!'

'We need to know for sure!'

Decimus grabbed Olu by the arm and dragged him towards the edge of the rocky path. Keeping a firm hold on his friend's arm, he crept very quickly around the edge of the battle. The pair stopped only once on their careful journey towards the tower gates, to watch with bewildered awe as Slavious Doom hoisted one unfortunate slave into the air and hurled him at several others. Then they were on their way again, past struggling sentries and screaming slaves, over giant rocks and burning sand and, finally, through the great double doors that led to the tower courtyard.

Ruma descended the chain like a spider-monkey climbing down a tree. When he reached the very last link, he hung there for a moment, realized that he was still too far from the ground to let go and promptly began to swing back and forth in slow, determined sweeps, picking up speed as he went. After one final pass, he let go of the chain and swung out over the mostly distracted merchant crowd, crashing on to the roof of the scaffold and rolling over several times before slamming into an expanse of dirt directly in front of the audience. The pain ravaged his body, but he fought through it and leapt to his feet, screwing up his face and screaming like an enraged banshee at the wall of faces before him. This was too much for the merchant crowd who, noticing the sudden lack of guards around them, began to scramble to their feet and make for the exits.

Delighted at this reaction, Ruma quickly scampered over the edge of the stalls and leapt upon a stunned merchant, snatching the

man's dagger before taking a second, longer leap down on to the courtyard's main stage. A quick glimpse told him everything: Gladius was being taken apart by Drin Hain, but in a manner that suggested the assassin was intent on providing him with a slow death, while Argon had managed to evade the snake swarm and was already scampering up the side of the pit, a cascade of dirt flying in his wake. It was Teo who needed the help: the oriental slave was still kicking frantically, but his strength was visibly waning.

Ruma dashed for the stage.

As Decimus and Olu entered the tower courtyard, they were greeted by a horde of rampaging merchants. The group, which looked to be more than a hundred strong, were all visibly terrified, and washed over them like a great wave breaking over rocks: not one of them looked back. Decimus and Olu both drew their swords, and advanced.

Ruma had failed to raise the trapdoor beneath Teo's feet. Instead, he'd had to use an old plank he'd found wedged against the lion cage, and was now balancing precariously over the hole while trying to lift Teo up in an attempt to take the pressure off his neck. Teo had stopped moving several seconds before, but Ruma was determined not to give up.

'Come on, Teo!' he yelled, his feet

scrambling for purchase on the wood. 'Don't
you die on me!'

Gladius raised his sword and tried to lunge
at Drin Hain, who side-stepped the clumsy
assault and brought his own blade down in a
swift arc. Steel met steel and, to Gladius's
surprise, his sword was shattered. He
stepped back and looked down at the broken
hilt in his hands, but the shadow continued
to stalk him. A fist flew out of the cloak like
a rock and slammed into his face: he felt
blood begin to flow from his nose, and tasted
the sweet liquid as it dripped on to his
tongue. Hain didn't stop there: a second blow
doubled him over, and a knee was driven

into the side of his face. The world flew away, and Gladius hit the dirt; hard.

Hain released a pitying cackle, and raised his sword to finish him. Then, wanting to take a moment to make the final strike worthy of an expectant crowd, he quickly glanced around him . . . at a very different scene.

The merchants had all rushed for the doors, where it looked as though a larger, separate struggle was taking place. Slavious Doom was nowhere to be seen, and the gangly Etrurian slave was attempting to save his friend from the noose by balancing over the trapdoor and lifting him up. As Hain tried to decide where his attention was most urgently required, a shrill whistle at his shoulder shook him from his reverie. He spun around . . . and Decimus Rex plunged a sword straight into his heart.

Argon was running out of energy in his bid to escape the pit. The walls were too rough; every time he made some sort of progress, he slipped back down amid an avalanche of dirt. To make matters worse, several of the smaller snakes had bitten his legs . . . and a network of pain was beginning to creep through his body. His legs felt like dead weights.

Putting on one final burst of energy, Argon scraped, clawed and heaved his way up the side of the pit.

Then . . . all at once . . . he could do no more.

His eyes fixed on the light and the noise above, he could only watch himself slowly slip back into the writhing furore of the snake pit.

Argon closed his eyes, prayed to his god . . . and let himself fall.

A hand closed around his wrist.

Argon started, and his eyes flicked open. He found himself staring at a very familiar face: Olu had a smile that was simply unforgettable.

'Come on!' said the slave, hauling his friend out of the depths. 'I thought you Gauls were supposed to be strong.'

Argon spat out an entire mouthful of abuse, but he also found an extra reserve of strength. He and Olu rolled on to the stage and tried to get to their feet, but, as they did so, they were greeted by a truly dreadful sight . . .

Ruma was sitting on the ground beside the trapdoor, rocking backwards and forwards in the dirt. His eyes were streaming with tears, and his entire body was shaking. Above him, Teo hung motionless from the scaffold: he was dead.

Drin Hain staggered back, his hood falling away to reveal a plain and unmarked face that was full of surprise, confusion and anger.

Decimus gritted his teeth and stepped forward, driving his elbow into the assassin's jaw and knocking him to the ground.

Drin Hain, great killer of slaves and shadowy apprentice to Slavious Doom, curled up like a newborn baby and clutched at the sword that protruded from his stomach. His eyes flickered for a moment, and then focused in a terrible, distant stare.

Decimus stepped around the fallen assassin, and moved over to crouch beside his friend.

'Gladius,' he said, speaking slowly and carefully. 'It's Decimus. Can you hear me?'

Gladius moved his head slightly. His breathing was measured, but he was out cold: his face was covered in blood from Hain's assault, and his lips trembled as if he was suffering the worst kind of nightmare.

At least he was alive.

As Decimus hauled the unconscious slave off the dirt, he glanced over at Argon and

Olu, who were helping Ruma to free Teo
from the noose. Decimus guessed from
Ruma's tear-streaked face that Teo was dead.
Now they were five.

Gladius was a heavy burden. Decimus
looped the big slave's arm around his neck
and tried to move him towards the edge of
the stage, but he soon froze.

On the opposite end of the scaffold, Ruma,

Olu and Argon were equally still. They had managed to get Teo's body to the ground, but Argon had spotted the scene unfolding around them and had alerted the others.

Nobody moved.

Around the edge of the tower courtyard, some twenty guards surrounded them. Some were armed with swords, many with spears and a few carried the deadly combination of trident and net. All were advancing towards them, poised for combat.

Slavious Doom strode through the great doors and held up an armoured hand.

'Wait!' he cried, pointing across the courtyard as he approached the gathered slaves. 'Will you look at this: the great Decimus Rex has returned ... precisely as

Hain predicted. His plan worked beautifully ... such a pity he will not be around to see it bear fruit.' Slavious stared down at his fallen apprentice, but he didn't look even remotely concerned. His attention quickly shifted back to the young gladiator. 'Now, you are mine once again.'

Decimus felt himself begin to shake with anger, but he knew that any strike against the overlord would be futile. They were impossibly outnumbered, and Doom fought like a lion: from what Decimus had seen, the overlord was equivalent in strength to ten men.

'You didn't really presume that a handful of ship slaves would be any match for me?' Doom continued. 'Oh certainly, we suffered some losses . . . and I doubt the merchants will be happy unless we return their precious money . . . but then I see you have your own small . . . hmm . . . disappointments?'

The armoured giant nodded at Teo's corpse, and it took the combined efforts of Argon and Olu to keep Ruma from racing at him.

'You will suffer more losses if I advance now,' said Doom, his voice almost casual. 'I can get my men to cut down your friends, leaving you utterly alone to face my wrath.'

Decimus raised his sword as the guards began to move forward, but he knew they really didn't stand a chance.

Doom's face was consumed by a sickly, almost demonic smile.

'I'm not going to kill any of your friends now,' he boomed, as yet another group of guards arrived at the gates. 'For they will be far more useful to me back at Arena Primus . . . as bargaining tools.'

'Bargaining tools?' questioned Argon. He, Ruma and Olu were all staring over at Decimus, whose own expression indicated that he didn't have the slightest clue what Slavious Doom was referring to.

'Bargaining tools against whom?' Decimus shouted, as he felt Gladius begin to stir.

Doom released a sardonic cackle. 'Against you, my boy. This entire event was arranged to bring YOU back to me. Did you believe I arranged all of this simply to stop two ordinary slaves escaping my grasp? Hahaha!

MANY slaves have escaped me over the years, my young friends, and I can assure you I made no such efforts to recapture them. You are special, Decimus; it is a pure and simple fact. I need you to complete a task for me – a task that you alone are able to complete . . . a task that is your DESTINY.'

'I would kill myself before I helped you do anything,' Decimus spat.

Slavious Doom shrugged.

'Then do it now,' he yelled. 'For you will watch your friends suffer and die one by one unless you do exactly as I command.'

In the pensive silence, Doom turned and strode from the courtyard.

'Take them back to Arena Primus,' he boomed. 'ALL of them.'

COMING SOON

Decimus Rex is once more back in the clutches of the evil Slavious Doom. Tasked with entering the catacombs beneath the arena to bring back the fabled Blade of Fire, Decimus immediately demands the release of all his friends in return for agreeing to take on the mission. Doom, however, has other plans ...

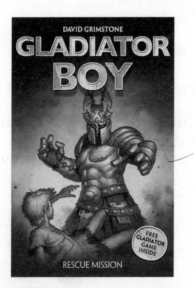

RESCUE MISSION

ARENA COMBAT

Get ready to challenge your friends! Each Gladiator Boy book will contain a different trial – collect them all to run your own Arena of Doom!

TRIAL 4
THE BITE

In this book, one of the young slaves meets a grizzly fate and all of the others escape theirs only by the narrowest of margins.
It all seems to come down to luck in the end.

You will need either two, three or four players, ten pieces of paper – all the same size – and a container or box of some kind.

In this trial, the players

imagine themselves walking through a room full of snakes. Most of the snakes are harmless, but one is poisonous – if the players are bitten, they are eliminated and lose the trial.

GAME PROCEDURE

One selected player writes the word 'harmless' on nine of the pieces of paper. He then writes the word 'poisonous' on the remaining one piece.

The pieces of paper are then placed into the box.

Decide who will go first by flipping a coin

The first player dips his hand into the box and draws out a piece of paper. If he draws the word 'harmless', he keeps hold of the piece of paper and the next player takes a turn. If he draws the word 'poisonous', he puts the piece of paper back into the case and is eliminated from the game. Play then passes to the next player.

The last player remaining in the game is the winner of the trial!

CHARACTER PROFILE
RUMA

NAME: Ruma

FROM: Etruria

HEIGHT: 1.70 metres

BODY TYPE: Scrawny, rough-skinned

BEST FRIEND: Teo

CELLMATE: Olu

RUMA QUIZ: How well do you know Ruma? Can you answer the following questions?

1. RUMA IS THE FIRST PERSON TO ASSUME GLADIUS HAS DIED IN THE UNDERWATER CHALLENGE. TRUE OR FALSE?

2. RUMA WAS THE ONLY SLAVE NOT TO HAVE HIS HEAD COVERED DURING THE EXECUTIONS. WHAT DID HE NOT HAVE TO WEAR?

Answers: 1. True, page 25 2. A cloth sack, page 64

WEAPON
PROFILE
THE FLAIL

A flail consists of a wooden handle attached
to a chain with a spiked ball on the end. It can
be swung at enemies, and also used to wrap
around the swords of opponents in order to
block their attacks. The flail makes a
whooshing noise when it is whirled through
the air, and can be swung at high speed over
the head of the wielder. It is a particularly
effective weapon when being attacked from
all sides!

READ MORE OF DECIMUS REX'S ADVENTURES IN BOOK FIVE OF THE GLADIATOR BOY SERIES:

RESCUE MISSION

Decimus had been confined in a small cell for six days. It wasn't any old cell, he realized upon entering, but the same dusty room he had occupied during the trials. The trials now seemed so far in the past that they almost felt like stories he'd heard from someone else. However, there was one major difference this time; the rest of the cell block was empty. Decimus hadn't seen Olu, Ruma, Argon or Gladius since they'd been captured in the courtyard of Suvius Tower. At first, he'd fully expected the group to be separated. They were obviously stronger together, and the simple fact that Doom had used the others as a trap to capture him and Olu meant that they were valuable to him. At least, that is the story Decimus told himself . . .

GLADIATOR BOY

Check out the Gladiator Boy website for games, downloads, activities, sneak previews and lots of fun! You can even get extra pieces of the arena and fantastic action figures! Sign up to the newsletter to receive exclusive extra content and the opportunity to enter special competitions.

WWW.GLADIATORBOY.COM

LET BATTLE COMMENCE!

MAKE YOUR OWN ARENA OF DOOM

1. Carefully cut around the outline of the arena section. Ask an adult to help if necessary.
2. Fold across line A. Use a ruler to get a straight edge.
3. Fold across line B. Use a ruler to get a straight edge.
4. Ask an adult to help you score along lines C & D with a pair of sharp scissors.
5. Fold up over line E and push the window out.
6. Repeat instructions 1 to 5 for every Arena of Doom piece collected.
7. Glue the top of each tab and stick them to the next piece of the arena. Repeat as necessary.

CHECK OUT THE WEBSITE FOR A PHOTO OF THE COMPLETE ARENA.

TO MAKE YOUR ACTION FIGURE

1. Cut around the outline of the figure. Ask an adult to help if necessary.
2. Cut along slot X at the bottom of the figure.
3. Cut out Gladiator Boy rectangle.
4. Cut along slot Y.
5. Slot figure into slot Y.